Dear Reader,

The true story of *Night of the Moonjellies* began many summers ago with a little boy, his grandmother's popular seaside hot dog stand and a mysterious blob of jelly.

I was the boy, of course, and my remembrance of that wonderful day ends after just a few pages with a surprise. But the story of this book and how it found its readers has been quite a surprise as well.

Published first in 1992, *Night of the Moonjellies* seemed destined for oblivion. After only a few short years it was discontinued by the publisher and disappeared into the vast sea of out of print works in the book business.

But thousands of children and almost as many adults found something special in this story and I am forever grateful to them.

Their hundreds of letters over the last ten years, the unceasing demand from folks in the international organization Five In A Row, and my new friends at Purple House Press have brought *Night of the Moonjellies* back.

It seems this little book has finally found the place where it belongs, not unlike a certain small jellyfish I once knew.

Thank you,
Mark Shasha

Dear Reader,

The true story of Night of the Moonjellies began many summers ago with a little boy, his grandmother's popular seaside hot dog stand and a mysterious blob of jelly.

I was the boy, of course, and my remembrance of that wonderful day ends after just a few pages with a surprise. But the story of this book and how it found its readers has been quite a surprise as well.

Published first in 1992, Night of the Moonjellies seemed destined for oblivion. After only a few short years it was discontinued by the publisher and disappeared into the vast sea of out of print works in the book business.

But thousands of children and almost as many adults found something special in this story and I am forever grateful to them.

Their hundreds of letters over the last ten years, the unceasing demand from folks in the international organization Five in A Row, and my new friends at Purple House Press have brought Night of the Moonjellies back.

It seems this little book has finally found the place where it belongs, not unlike a certain small jellyfish I once knew.

Thank you,
Mark Shasha

NIGHT OF THE
MOONJELLIES

Mark Shasha

NIGHT OF THE MOONJELLIES

PURPLE HOUSE PRESS Texas

The summer I was seven I helped out two days a week at Mar-Gra's, a seaside hot dog stand that made the best lobster rolls in New England. It was named after the owners, my grandmother Mary and her sister Grace.

One Friday morning, I woke up at Gram's and grabbed my apron on the way out the door. Along the beach I picked up pieces of sea glass, worn and rounded by the ocean. Then I found something that felt like jelly. I put it in a plastic bag with the sea glass, poured in some seawater, and ran the rest of the way to Mar-Gra's.

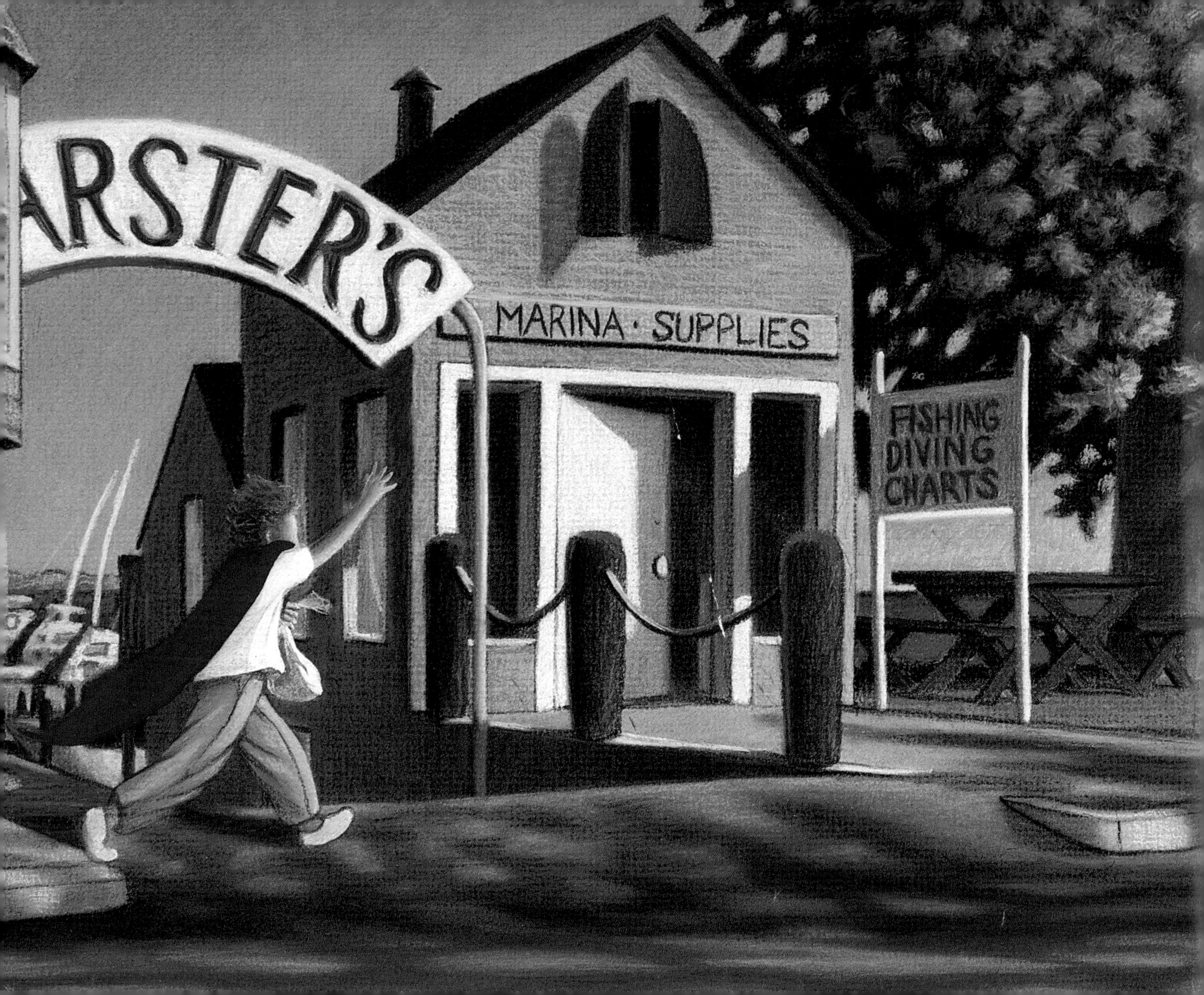
ARSTER'S
MARINA · SUPPLIES
FISHING
DIVING
CHARTS

Gram was already there, getting the stand ready for opening. She hugged me and a puff of flour rose up from her apron.

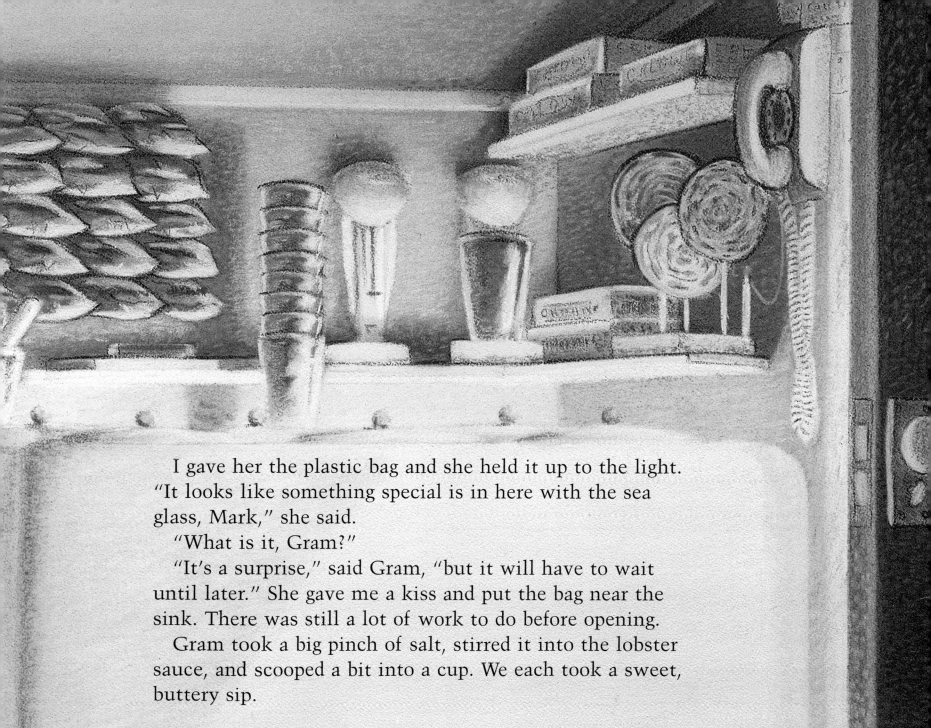

I gave her the plastic bag and she held it up to the light. "It looks like something special is in here with the sea glass, Mark," she said.

"What is it, Gram?"

"It's a surprise," said Gram, "but it will have to wait until later." She gave me a kiss and put the bag near the sink. There was still a lot of work to do before opening.

Gram took a big pinch of salt, stirred it into the lobster sauce, and scooped a bit into a cup. We each took a sweet, buttery sip.

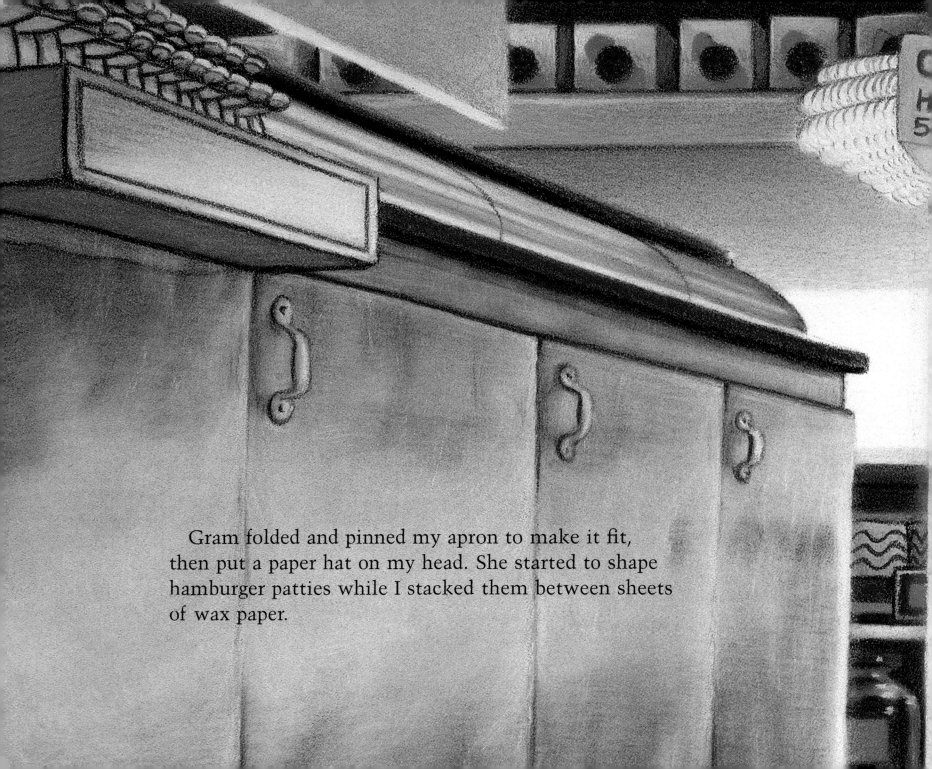

Gram folded and pinned my apron to make it fit,
then put a paper hat on my head. She started to shape
hamburger patties while I stacked them between sheets
of wax paper.

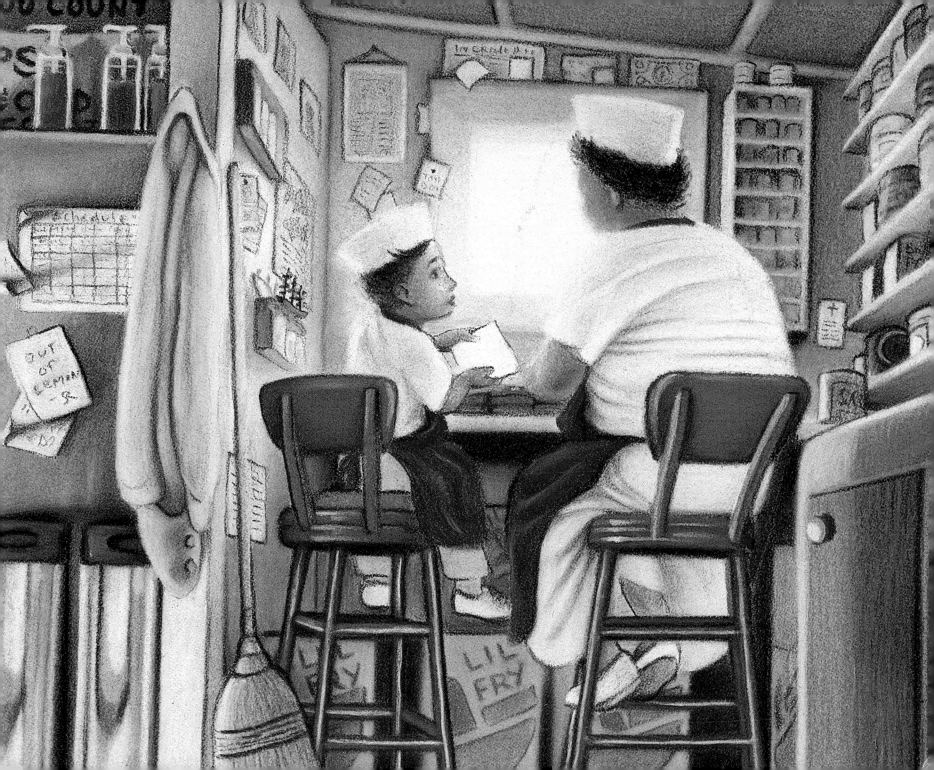

"Good morning, you two," boomed Uncle Al. He switched on the grill and sprinkled it with slices of pepper and onion.

Gram started the fried clams while I checked the catsup, mustard, and relish jars. I was also in charge of straws and napkins.

Aunt Grace walked in tying her apron just as the first customers drove up.

Cousin Rollie appeared around the corner with a stack of umbrellas on his shoulder. I cranked them open as he dropped them into the holes in the tables. Behind us the stand had filled.

"Three lobster rolls! Two orange sodas! Burger! Three fries! Two chocolate shakes!"

Fries crackled. Cheeseburgers sizzled.

"More rolls!" called Uncle Al.

"Rushing through!" Gram said, carrying a kettle of clam chowder up front.

"Low on straws!" Rollie shouted.

I hurried to fill the box.

Finally, the seats facing the water were empty again.

"Let's have lunch while we can," Gram said, bringing over a tray of lobster rolls and onion rings.

We ate where we could watch the boats.

"I think it'll be even busier tonight," Gram said, "and we're out of onion rings."

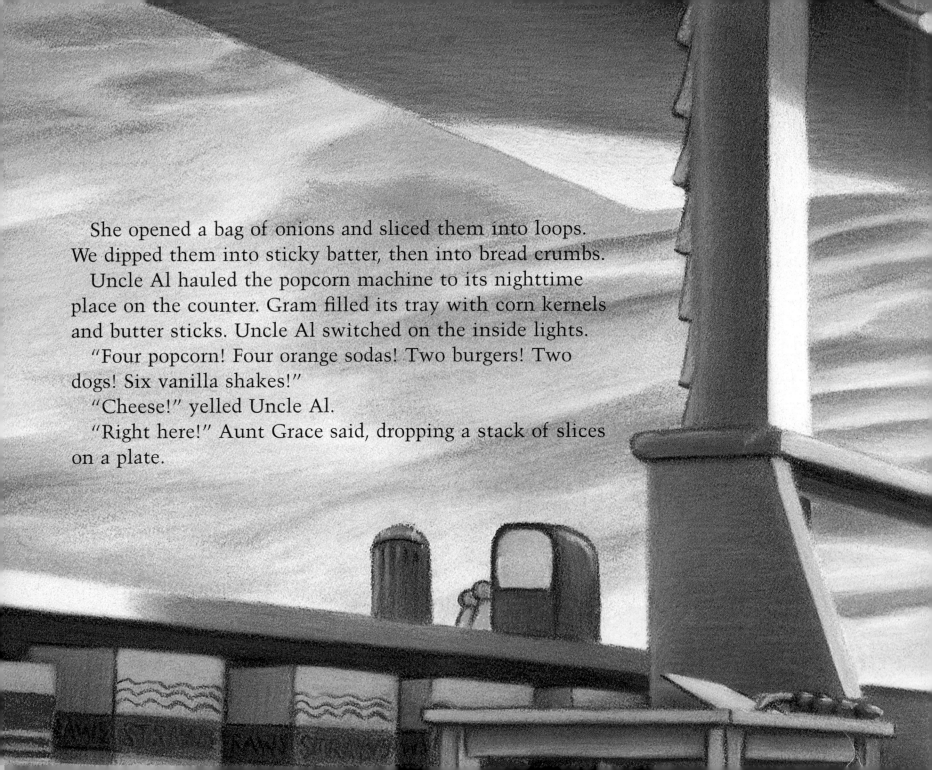

She opened a bag of onions and sliced them into loops.
We dipped them into sticky batter, then into bread crumbs.

Uncle Al hauled the popcorn machine to its nighttime
place on the counter. Gram filled its tray with corn kernels
and butter sticks. Uncle Al switched on the inside lights.

"Four popcorn! Four orange sodas! Two burgers! Two
dogs! Six vanilla shakes!"

"Cheese!" yelled Uncle Al.

"Right here!" Aunt Grace said, dropping a stack of slices
on a plate.

Customers crowded the counter. Radios blared baseball and music. Horns beeped.

"Catsup's low!" shouted Uncle Al.

"Lobster rolls ready!" Gram called.

Pots clanged. The register rang. Customers waved as they drove off. I ate a cheeseburger. It was a busy, noisy night.

When the last customers left, it was time to begin the night chores. Uncle Al scrubbed the grill to a silvery shine. Gram washed the pots and utensils. I helped her dry them and put them away. Rollie collected the umbrellas. The counter workers went home.

"Good-night, you two," Uncle Al said as he locked the stand. He hugged us and drove off in the moonlight, leaving us with the sounds of crickets and rustling leaves.

Gram handed me a sweater. "You'll need this for the surprise," she said.

She started down the pier and stopped at a boat, the
Periwinkle.

"Welcome aboard!" said a cheery voice.

Tyler, a fisherman, helped us onto the boat. "There's hot
chocolate inside," he said.

Tyler threw the ropes onto the dock and climbed up to
start the engine. The engine roared as we headed out to
the dark sea.

"Let's go in and keep warm," Gram said.

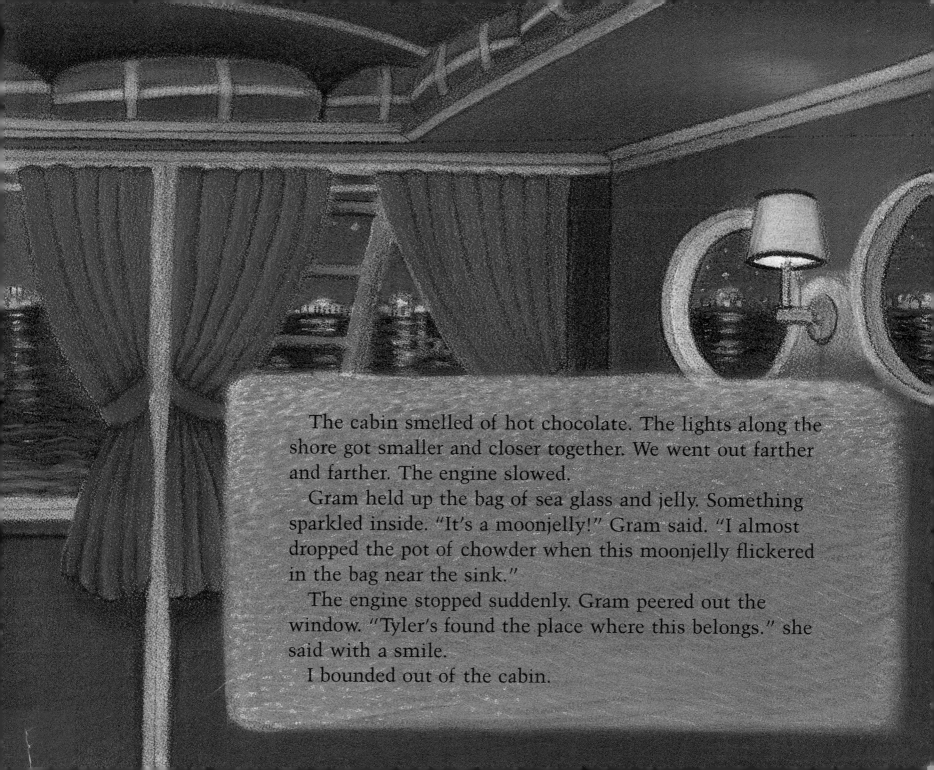

The cabin smelled of hot chocolate. The lights along the shore got smaller and closer together. We went out farther and farther. The engine slowed.

Gram held up the bag of sea glass and jelly. Something sparkled inside. "It's a moonjelly!" Gram said. "I almost dropped the pot of chowder when this moonjelly flickered in the bag near the sink."

The engine stopped suddenly. Gram peered out the window. "Tyler's found the place where this belongs." she said with a smile.

I bounded out of the cabin.

Thousands of moonjellies stretched along the sea in
every direction.
   I opened the bag and poured out our moonjelly. Now it
was with the others. We stood on the deck and watched the
shimmering sea.

After a while Tyler started the engine and we headed home.

At the dock we thanked Tyler and walked to Gram's. She made chamomile tea and put some melon on a plate.

She held up the pieces of sea glass to the light, then put them into a small box. She was writing something on the box when my eyes began to close. It read, "With love to Mark from Gram — night of the moonjellies."

AUTHOR'S NOTE

The scientific name for the small, colorless creature in this story is Ctenophore, pronounced *tee´ ne for*. Moonjellies are also called comb jellies or sea gooseberries. They usually grow no larger than a child's fist and in New England are most plentiful in late summer. They are not actually true jellyfish because they don't have stinging cells or tentacles. Moonjellies are harmless.

They are also bioluminescent, meaning they are able to create light, like fireflies, with chemical reactions in their bodies. Like true jellyfish, ctenophores are made up mostly of water. There is a true jellyfish in the sea named Moon Jellyfish, its scientific name is *Aurelia aurita*. Though quite nice to look at, it has tentacles, stinging cells and is not bioluminescent. It is a good deal larger than a ctenophore, and it is not the jellyfish of *Night of the Moonjellies*.

Mar-Gra's was a busy seaside diner at 272 Pequot Avenue in New London, Connecticut from 1956 to 1971. It was owned by my grandmother Mary Shasha and her sister Grace Steadman; it was open from early spring to late fall. Almost all of my extended family worked at Mar-Gra's at one time or another. It was usually open late and was well-known for great hamburgers, foot–long hot dogs, and of course, delicious lobster rolls.

Mary was an especially beloved and active person in New London. Members of her church groups and ladies societies would often gather at the picnic tables beside the docks and elm tree to sip coffee or tea. She managed to laugh and chat with a steady stream of visitors while she worked, always making sure to thank every customer.

In 1972 the business moved across the street into a new building with a dining room and an expanded menu which even included Neapolitan pizza with the hopes of staying open year round. The move proved too expensive and Mar-Gra's closed in 1977.

With love to Mom and Dad — MS

PURPLE HOUSE PRESS
1625 Village Trail, Keller, TX 76248
Copyright © 1992 by Mark Shasha. Foreword, Afterword and new illustration copyright © 2002 by Mark Shasha.
All rights reserved.

Library of Congress Cataloging-in-Publication Data
Shasha, Mark.
Night of the moonjellies / by Mark Shasha. Summary: Seven-year-old Mark helps his grandmother and other family members run their seaside hot dog stand and then has a surprise at the end of the day.
[1. Restaurants, lunch rooms, etc. — Fiction. 2. Beaches — Fiction. 3. Grandmothers — Fiction.] I. Title
PZ7.S5324Su 2002 [E]—dc21 2001097700   ISBN 1-930900-16-3

www. PurpleHousePress.com   www.MarkShasha.com

Printed in South Korea
1 2 3 4 5 6 7 8 9 10